MW00928734

A DOG
AND
HIS BONE

by Mister Brock

Illustrated by Stephen Low

ISBN-13: 978-1-948026-18-5
E-book ISBN 13: 978-1-948026-19-2

Published by TMP Books, 3 Central Plaza, Ste 307, Rome, GA 30161

www.TMPbooks.com

Published in the United States of America.

When Rufus woke up...

...it was time to eat.

His master threw his bone like he did every day...

...but this time it soared
so very far away!

He searched 'til he found his bone near the shore.

Then Rufus spotted a friend he'd never played with before!

And as Rufus watched his friend fly off,
something else caught his eye!

He had found his bone,
but now found something more.
Three shiny new toys sitting on the sandy floor.

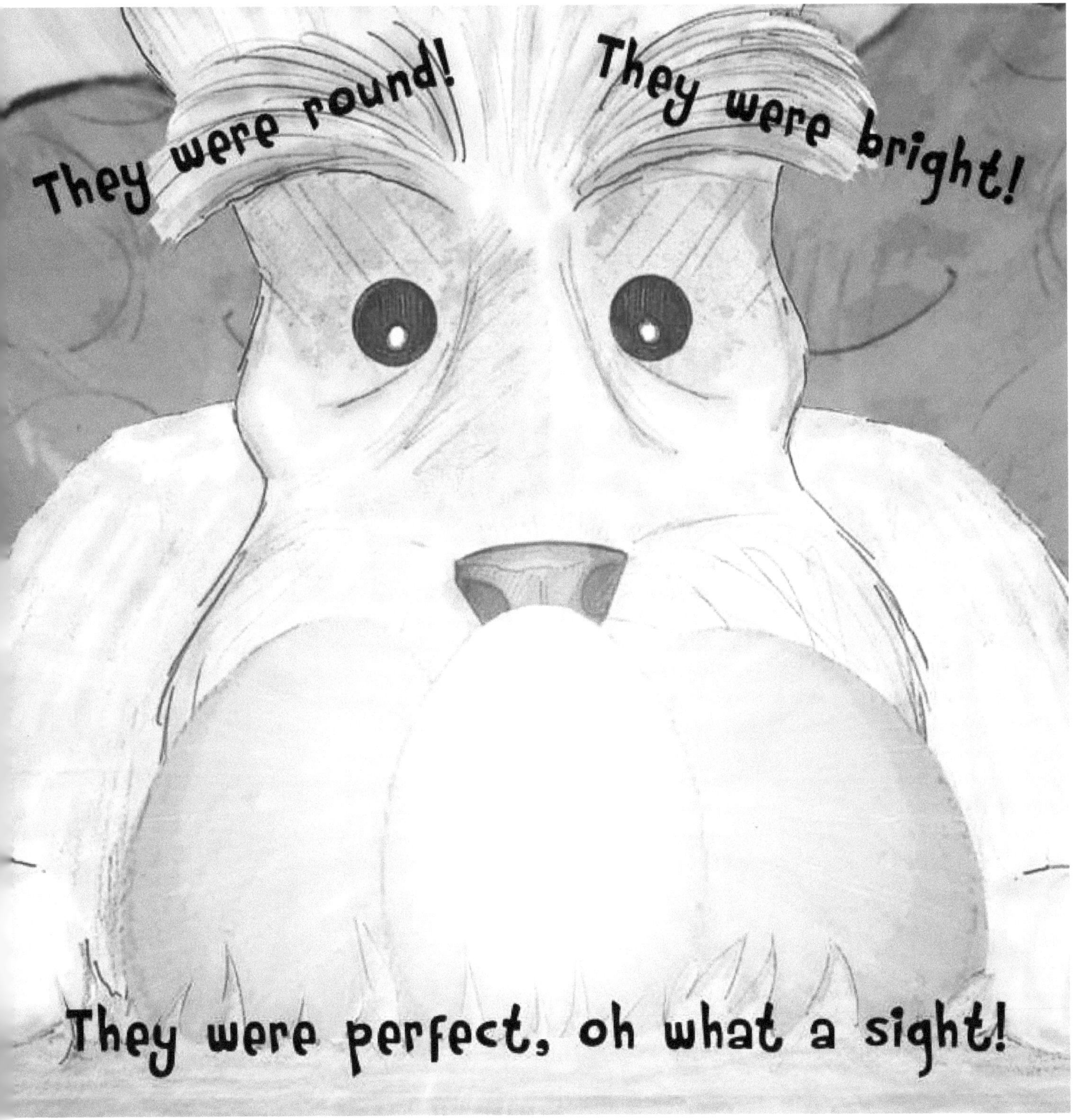

They were round! They were bright!

They were perfect, oh what a sight!

Then out of the sky came a pushing sound...

...as a large and proud heron began circling around!

"These are mine!"

Rufus barked with a snarl and a bite.

Then out of the sky an eagle swooped down, looking eager to play with the toys Rufus had found.

The eagle soared off,
taking the fish to her nest.

Where the three baby chicks ate,
before having a rest.

Then out of the blue, a turtle appeared.
With a smile on his face,
he snapped and he
sneered.

As the turtle swam off and the sun went down,
Rufus glanced at his toys with a most puzzled frown.

They SPLIT!

They CRINKLED!

They started to CRACK!

They ROLLED!

They RUMBLED!

They...

...started to quack?!

Then his friend from before swooped down into land, blocking the dog's view of the strangeness at hand.

"I'm a mother," She said. "So I protect my own."

"But you startled and scared me, so I left them alone."

"Thank you!"
Quacked Mother Duck
as she watched
Rufus go.

He had protected her babies without realising so.

The toys were now ducklings, all feathery and small.

...they could quack...

They could wiggle...

...they weren't toys at all.

Mother Duck now had a family,
thanks to a dog and his bone.

A dog whose own family was
now glad to have him home.

But still each
day Rufus wakes...

...and runs straight towards the shore.

Always hoping to find the toys that he had played with before.

But he sees only ducks,
all quacking away.

Saying 'thank you'
to Rufus for what
he did that day.

About the Author and Illustrator

Mister Brock (l) and Stephen Low (r)

Mister Brock and Stephen Low met in 2010 when they were both teachers in South Korea. Though one came from America and liked to write and the other called England his home and was a gifted artist, the two shared a passion for storytelling and creativity which led them to begin the process of creating A Dog and His Bone. Over the years, the two merged their talents and created the company "The Slow Connection," which has published numerous children's books for the teaching company VIPKID along with a number of other freelance projects. The two continue to create works together and remain close friends to this very day.

Visit them on the Web: **www.TheSlowConnection.net**.

Thank you for purchasing this book.

If you enjoyed it, please consider
leaving a brief review on Amazon or Goodreads.

Look for other books
published by

www.TMPbooks.com

CPSIA information can be obtained
at www.ICGtesting.com
Printed in the USA
BVHW020855181118
533396BV00035B/265/P

* 9 7 8 1 9 4 8 0 2 6 1 8 5 *